F is for FRIENDS
An Alphabet Book

By Mary Man-Kong
Illustrated by John Skewes

A GOLDEN BOOK • NEW YORK

Published in the United States by Golden Books, an imprint of Random House Children's Books, a division of Penguin Random House LLC, 1745 Broadway, New York, NY 10019, and in Canada by Penguin Random House Canada Limited, Toronto. Golden Books, A Golden Book, A Little Golden Book, the G colophon, and the distinctive gold spine are registered trademarks of Penguin Random House LLC.
rhcbooks.com
ISBN 978-0-593-80899-3 (trade) — ISBN 978-0-593-80900-6 (ebook)
Printed in the United States of America
10 9 8 7 6 5 4 3 2 1

A is for apartment, where the friends hang out.

B is for ball.
Joey and Ross like
to toss it around
for hours.

C is for couch,
where the gang drinks coffee at
Central Perk. **Delicious!**

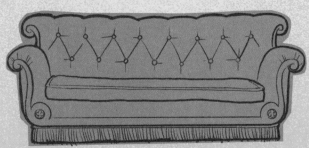

D is for dinosaurs.
Professor Ross Geller knows
all about dinosaurs.

RrROAR!!

E is for the eighties.
The friends went to college
during the eighties.

G is for Gunther. He works at Central Perk—
so he can be near Rachel. **Silly Gunther!**

H is for Halloween. The
gang dress up as Catwoman,
Supergirl, a bunny, and
Spudnik!

I is for ice. Phoebe makes sure there's plenty at the party.

Brrrr . . .

K

J is for jam. Monica makes jars of jam, and Joey eats some.

Yum!

K is for the keyboard that Ross plays—badly.

L is for lobsters,
who stay together for life—
just like Ross and Rachel. AWWWW!

M is for Marcel,
Ross's mischievous monkey.

N is for nap.
Ross and Joey take
the best nap ever.

O is for Oklahoma.
Chandler falls asleep and
accidentally accepts a job in his
company's Oklahoma office.

Zzzzz . . .

Tulsa is the Paris of Oklahoma.

P is for pivot.
This is what Ross shouts when
he, Rachel, and Chandler try to
maneuver his couch
up the stairs.

Q is for the quiz that Rachel fails when she gets a word wrong— and the girls lose their apartment to the boys.

R is for routine.
Monica and Ross do their old middle-school
dance routine to get on TV.

S is for "Smelly Cat,"
Phoebe's funny song.

U is for unagi,
which Ross believes is the state of being totally
prepared. (But he's not.)

Danger!

V is for vests—
as in sweater vests.
Chandler wants to bring only his
sweater vests to sunny Las Vegas.

Oh, Chandler!

W is for wearing. Chandler hides all of Joey's clothes, so Joey does the exact opposite—and wears all of Chandler's clothes!

I'm going commando!

X is for X-ray,
which Rachel needs
after she falls from
the balcony while
taking down the
X-mas lights.
Aaaah!

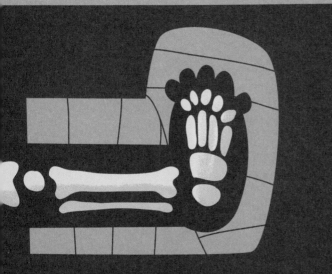

Y is for yeti,
which the girls fog
with a bug bomb.

That's our
neighbor
Danny!

Z is for zone. Ross is happy to be out of the friend zone when he and Rachel finally fall in love! But Monica, Ross, Rachel, Chandler, Joey, and Phoebe will always be great

FRIENDS!